THE THREE BILLY GOATS GRUFF

retold by Judith Smith and Brenda Parkes
illustrated by Mary Davy

Once upon a time
there were three Billy Goats Gruff.
There was a little Billy Goat Gruff,
and a middle-sized Billy Goat Gruff,
and a great big Billy Goat Gruff.

The three Billy Goats Gruff
lived on a hillside,
but they did not have enough to eat.
Over the bridge on another hill,
the grass was green and sweet.
But under the bridge lived
a bad-tempered Troll.

3

The Troll would not let the goats
cross the bridge.
The three Billy Goats Gruff grew
hungrier and **HUNGRIER.**
One day they were **so** hungry
they decided
to cross the bridge.

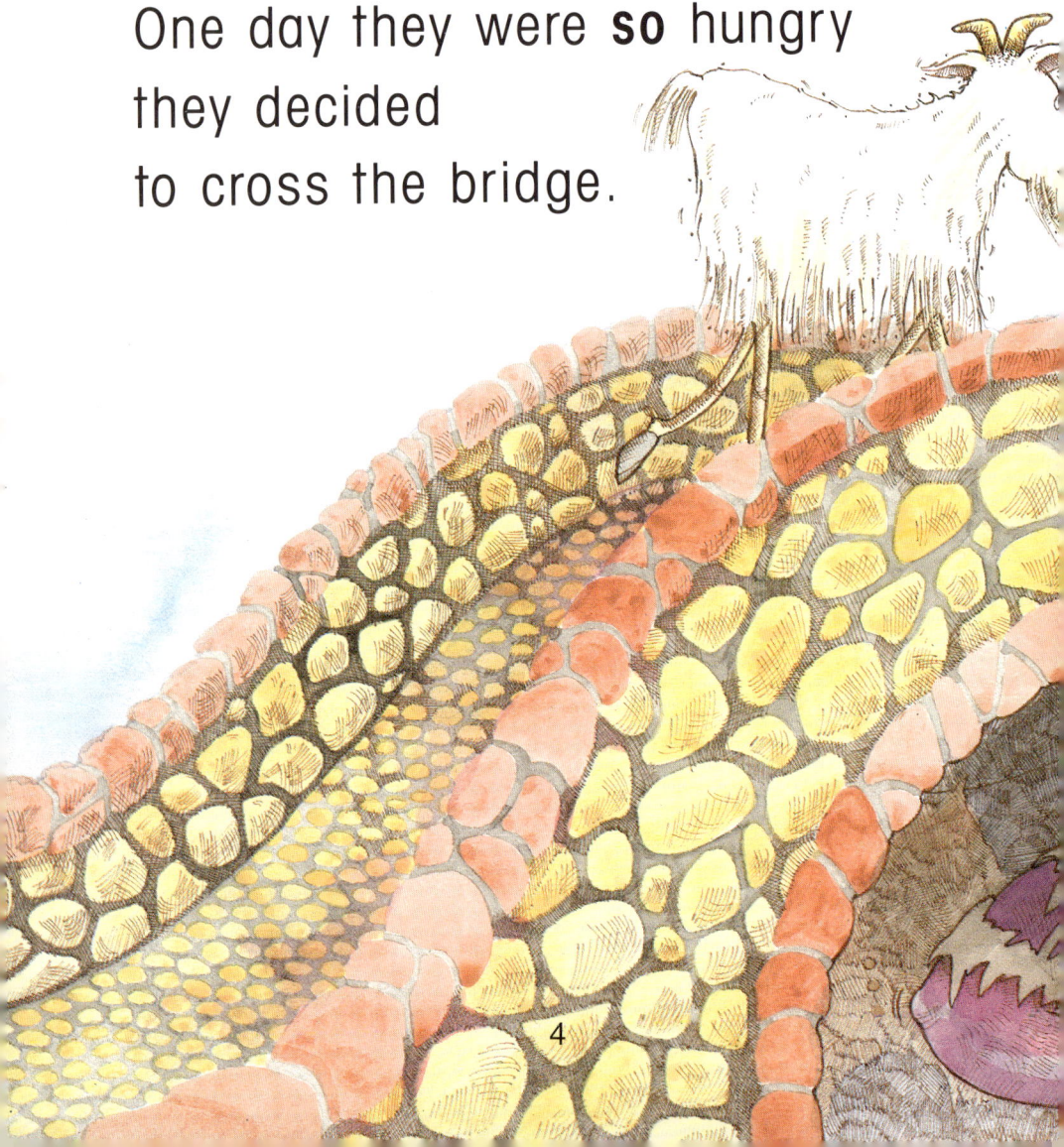

Little Billy Goat Gruff went first,

Trip trap trip trap

over the bridge.

**"WHO'S THAT CROSSING
OVER MY BRIDGE?"**
said the Troll.

"'Tis only I, the littlest Billy Goat Gruff," called the first Billy Goat Gruff.

"I'M GOING TO COME AND EAT YOU UP!" roared the Troll.

"OH! Please don't eat me.
Wait for my brother,
the middle-sized
Billy Goat Gruff.
He's much bigger than
I am," replied
Little Billy Goat Gruff.

"Oh! Very well!
Then be off with you,"
said the Troll.

8

The little Billy Goat ran away
and ate the sweet green grass.

Middle-sized Billy Goat Gruff
went next,

Trip trap trip trap

over the bridge.

"WHO'S THAT CROSSING OVER MY BRIDGE?"

said the Troll.

"'Tis only I,
the middle-sized
Billy Goat Gruff," called
the second Billy Goat Gruff.
**"I'M GOING TO COME
AND EAT YOU UP!"**
roared the Troll.

"OH! Please don't eat me.
Wait for my brother, Great
Big Billy Goat Gruff.
He's much bigger than
I am," replied Middle-sized
Billy Goat Gruff.

"Oh! Very well!
Then be off with you,"
said the Troll.

14

The middle-sized
Billy Goat Gruff
ran away and ate
the sweet green grass.

Then Great Big Billy Goat Gruff
began to cross the bridge.
He was big and mean and **hungry.**

Trip trap trip trap

over the bridge.

16

"WHO'S THAT CROSSING OVER MY BRIDGE?"
said the Troll.

"'Tis I, Great Big
Billy Goat Gruff," shouted
the third Billy Goat Gruff.

"I'M GOING TO COME AND EAT YOU UP!" roared the Troll.

He climbed up on to the bridge.

The great big Billy Goat
stopped still.
DOWN went his horns,
and he rushed at the Troll.
He butted him *once*

twice

three times.

The Troll tumbled off
the bridge,

down

down

down

into the deep water
under the bridge.

The great big Billy Goat went

Trip trap trip trap

over the bridge

and up the hill.

Soon he was eating
the sweet green grass.

The three Billy Goats Gruff
lived happily ever after.
They always had plenty to eat,
and no one has ever seen
the Troll again.